First U.S. edition 2005

Library of Congress Cataloging-in-Publication Data.

Puttapipat, Niroot.
The musicians of Bremen / retold and illustrated by Niroot Puttapipat. — 1st U.S. ed.
p.   cm.
Summary: While on their way to Bremen, four aging animals who are no longer of any use to their masters find a new home after outwitting a gang of robbers.
ISBN 0-7636-2758-5
[1. Fairy Tales. 2. Folklore—Germany.] I. Bremen town musicians. English. II. Title.
PZ8.P983Mu 2002
398.2 — dc22
[E]   2005046907

2 4 6 8 10 9 7 5 3 1

Printed in China

This book was typeset in Centaur and Zapfino.
The illustrations were done in watercolor and ink.

Candlewick Press
2067 Massachusetts Avenue
Cambridge, Massachusetts 02140

visit us at www.candlewick.com

The Musicians of Bremen

A Brothers Grimm tale retold and illustrated by

Niroot Puttapipat

CANDLEWICK PRESS
CAMBRIDGE, MASSACHUSETTS

"*Well, my friends,*" said Donkey as she approached the hearth, "what music shall we play this evening?"

"Monteverdi!" crowed Rooster from the footstool.

Dog circled a few times before settling on the hearthrug, saying, "No, let's play something by a German composer—Schütz, perhaps?"

"Why not something by a woman!" said Donkey, brightening. "Hildegard of Bingen!"

"If I may suggest . . ." began Cat silkily. The others turned to him. "Instead of making music tonight, why not let Donkey tell us a story—our favorite?"

There was a chorus of agreement as the others looked expectantly at Donkey.

"All right," she said. With a smile, she began. . . .

For many years, Donkey worked tirelessly for

her master, carrying sacks of flour and many other things

to and from the mill and market. But there came a time when

she had finally grown too old to bear the heavy loads.

"There's no money in that old donkey anymore," said

the master. "She'll have to go."

Donkey didn't like the sound of this at all, so she ran away.

"I shall go to Bremen to become a musician!" she brayed.

Whom should she meet on the way but a forlorn-looking

dog panting on the road. "Are you hurt?" she asked.

The dog looked up at her dolefully and shook his head.

"I can't keep up with my master's hunting

pack as I used to. Because of this, he plans to kill me!

I've run away but don't have the heart to go any farther."

"Then come with me!" cried Donkey. "We'll go to

Bremen and become town musicians. I can play

my lute and you can beat your kettledrum!"

Dog gave a gleeful bark and joined her.

Soon they met a miserable cat by the side of the road.

"Don't look so mournful," Donkey said. "Whatever's the matter?"

"I'm not so young anymore," he sighed. "My teeth and claws are not what they were. I can no longer catch mice, so my mistress means to drown me. What am I to do?"

"Come with us, then," replied Donkey. "We're going to Bremen to make music and could do with a good serenader like you! Come and be the violinist to my lutenist and Dog's drummer."

Cat was delighted.

Now a trio, they continued on their way.

Before long, they came across a rooster perched

on a farmyard gate. He looked

utterly furious and was

crowing for all he

was worth.

"Oh, dear," said Donkey.

"What can be so wrong?"

"What's wrong?!" wailed the rooster.

"Only that the mistress of the

house is preparing to wring my

neck for Sunday lunch, despite

my prediction of fine weather

for Our Lady's Day today! So

now I'm making all the noise

I can while I'm still alive!"

"Then put it to better use," Donkey replied, "and come with us to Bremen. I'm a lutenist, Dog's a drummer, Cat's a violinist, and with a voice like that, you will make a fine tenor. We'll be the best troubadours the town has ever known!"

Rooster loved the idea. He joined them, and as a new quartet, they traveled together toward Bremen.

By nightfall, the
tired and hungry friends arrived at a forest. Dog

and Donkey settled under a tree while Cat and

Rooster took to the branches. From his perch at

the top, Rooster could see a light from a distant

house—this would certainly be a more welcome place

of rest. They crept toward it and found it was a little

cottage. Donkey peered in through a window. "It looks

like a band of robbers," she said.

"What else can you see?" urged the others.

"Why, there's a table groaning under the weight of good things to eat!" answered Donkey breathlessly.

"Grapes and pears, puddings and pies, roasted meats, and wine!"

Gasping with hunger, the animals put their

heads together and came up with a plan to seize

the cottage and its contents for themselves. First Donkey

stood with her hooves on the windowsill. Then Dog

jumped onto her neck. Cat pounced upon Dog's back,

and Rooster flew up to perch on Cat's head.

At a signal from Donkey, all at once they launched into

their music and crashed in through the window. Donkey

brayed the bass continuo, Dog drummed ferociously with

his barking, Cat provided counterpoint with the

meowing of his violin, while Rooster sang a

gloriously alarming aria! The robbers bolted

from the cottage. Terrified that a monster

had burst in, they ran into the woods.

The musicians gathered around the table and ate as though they'd never eat again. When every morsel was gone, they put out the light and found places to sleep.

Donkey settled into the
pile of straw in the yard,

Dog lay down behind
the cottage door,

Cat curled up by the fireside,

and Rooster flew
up into the rafters.

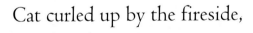

Meanwhile, the
robbers had been
keeping watch from the
woods, and the chief soon
sent one of his men back for their
loot. Finding the cottage in darkness,
the robber decided to strike a light. Cat, crouched by the
hearth, regarded him warily. The robber mistook his glowing
eyes for live coals and held a candle up to them. What
impertinence! thought Cat, and he leaped up, spitting and
scratching the robber's face. With a cry, the man stumbled
toward the door, whereupon Dog jumped up and sank
his teeth into the robber's leg.

The terrified man ran screaming into

the yard, and from there, Donkey sent him off

with an almighty kick.

As a finale, Rooster flew from the rafters to the

top of the cottage and cried, "Cock-a-doodle-doo!"

"Oh monstrous! Oh strange! We

are haunted!" the robber shrieked as

he staggered back to his gang.

The next day, the friends heard from a pair of pigeons a delightful tale of robbers fleeing a cottage that had been overrun by some truly terrifying beings.

One of the robbers had apparently been scratched viciously by a dreadful witch, stabbed in the leg by a troll, and then dealt a merciless blow by a demon with a club. What was more, on the roof sat the judge himself, bellowing, "And jail for you too!" as the man made his escape. It was said that the robbers vowed never to venture near the cottage again.

All that day, the four friends laughed and rejoiced at their success.

"The robbers never did return," said Rooster with satisfaction.

"Nor did we ever make it to Bremen, after all," murmured Dog.

"The cottage is so much to our liking," purred Cat.

"So here we are," sighed Donkey happily, "still making our wonderful music together."

The German "Bremen Town Musicians," included in the Grimm brothers' second edition of their *Children's and Household Tales* in 1819, is probably the best-known version of this tale, although there are many told throughout the world. One from Switzerland features a horse instead of a donkey and a goose instead of a rooster. There is also an interesting version from mid-nineteenth-century America, in which, as in the Swiss tale, the animals are not musicians. Here, the adventure is started by the dog, who simply grows tired of his guarding duties. His reluctant companions are persuaded to join him only when he warns them of their fates when they grow old.

The closest version to the Grimms' tale comes from Flanders. The animals' intended destination is the Cathedral of St. Gudule in Brussels, where they plan to become choristers (four *voices* rather than one voice and three instruments). In this tale, they good-naturedly hope to be rewarded for singing and only accidentally fall in through the window of the cottage — with satisfactory, if not quite the intended, results!

I have chosen to set my retelling in the early seventeenth century. This decision gave me the chance to mention a few great composers of the time and so strengthen the musical aspect of the story. Although some retellings have chosen the horn as the donkey's instrument, I think the lute's sounds are more suited to a donkey's braying and more in keeping with the music of the period.

The contemporaneous composers mentioned at the beginning of this story are Claudio Monteverdi (1567–1643), Italian composer of operas and church music, and Heinrich Schütz (1585–1672), from Germany. The exception to these composers is Hildegard von Bingen (1098–1179), a German nun and composer of plainchant and sacred music. Donkey mentions her because, of course, she too is female. I thought it was high time this tale featured a female as the leader of the group!

Niroot Puttapipat

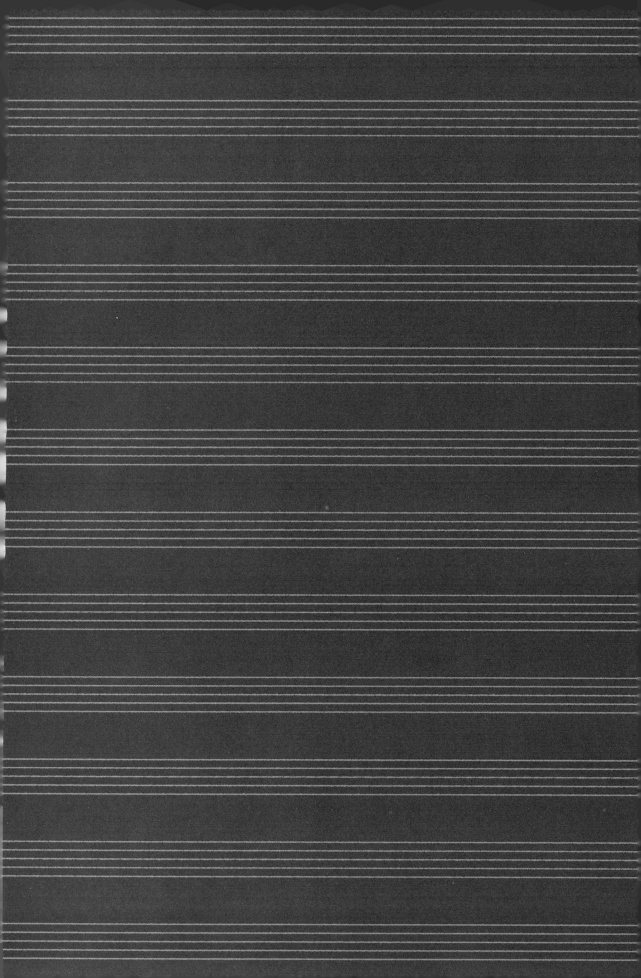